Hello, Family Members,

Learning to read is one of the most important accomplishments of early childhood. **Hello Reader!** books are designed to help children become skilled readers who like to read. Beginning readers learn to read by remembering frequently used words like "the," "is," and "and"; by using phonics skills to decode new words; and by interpreting picture and text clues. These books provide both the stories children enjoy and the structure they need to read fluently and independently. Here are suggestions for helping your child *before*, *during*, and *after* reading:

Before
- Look at the cover and pictures and have your child predict what the story is about.
- Read the story to your child.
- Encourage your child to chime in with familiar words and phrases.
- Echo read with your child by reading a line first and having your child read it after you do.

During
- Have your child think about a word he or she does not recognize right away. Provide hints such as "Let's see if we know the sounds" and "Have we read other words like this one?"
- Encourage your child to use phonics skills to sound out new words.
- Provide the word for your child when more assistance is needed so that he or she does not struggle and the experience of reading with you is a positive one.
- Encourage your child to have fun by reading with a lot of expression . . . like an actor!

After
- Have your child keep lists of interesting and favorite words.
- Encourage your child to read the books over and over again. Have him or her read to brothers, sisters, grandparents, and even teddy bears. Repeated readings develop confidence in young readers.
- Talk about the stories. Ask and answer questions. Share ideas about the funniest and most interesting characters and events in the stories.

I do hope that you and your child enjoy this book.

—Francie Alexander
Reading Specialist,
Scholastic's Instructional Publishing Group

If you have questions or comments about how children learn to read, please contact Francie Alexander at FrancieAl@aol.com

ISBN 0-590-12062-X

Copyright © 1998 Warner Bros.
QUEST FOR CAMELOT, characters, names, and all related indicia
are trademarks of Warner Bros.
All rights reserved. Published by Scholastic Inc.
Cover art © ARKADIA Illustration and Design Limited.
HELLO READER! and CARTWHEEL BOOKS and logos
are trademarks and/or registered trademarks of Scholastic Inc.

10 9 8 7 6 5 4 3 2 1   8 9/9 0/0 01 02

Book Design by Alfred Giuliani
Printed in the U.S.A.
First Scholastic printing, May 1998

23

Warner Bros.

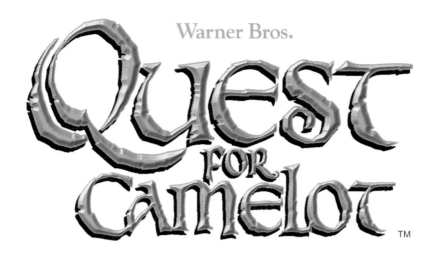

QUEST FOR CAMELOT ™

Hello Reader! — Level 3

SCHOLASTIC INC.

New York   Toronto   London   Auckland   Sydney

 INTRODUCTION

Long ago there was a land
with no king.
The people needed a ruler
to bring peace.
Their only hope lay in a sword
that was trapped in a rock.
Only the true king could pull
that sword from the stone.
The sword was called Excalibur.
And the boy who finally freed it
was called Arthur.
On that day, the kingdom
of Camelot was born.
With his Knights of the Round Table,
King Arthur brought peace and
happiness to the land.

Years later, the kingdom faced
an even greater challenge.
An evil man named Ruber wanted
to take over Camelot.
Once a Knight of the Round Table,
Ruber had grown greedy.
He wanted all of the wealth and power
of Camelot for himself.
Ruber sent a Griffin to attack the king.
The Griffin, part eagle and part lion,
badly wounded King Arthur.
The creature then took Excalibur.
With the king hurt and Excalibur lost,
Camelot was in great danger.
Who would save the kingdom this time?

CHAPTER ONE
Ruber

"Excalibur is missing," said Kayley.
"I must go after it."

Her mother, Juliana, sighed.

Kayley had always wanted to be
a knight.

Her father, Sir Lionel, had been
a Knight of the Round Table.

Kayley loved hearing tales of his
daring rescues and bravery.

But Lionel had been killed years before
by the evil Ruber.

And now, Excalibur was missing
and the king was wounded.

Juliana was not about to lose another
loved one.

"Finding Excalibur is a job
for the knights, not a young girl,"
said Juliana.
Before Kayley could answer,
the doors burst open.
Juliana and Kayley gasped as Ruber
entered the house.

Forcing them outside, he told
the women of his plot
to take over Camelot.
Ruber needed Juliana to sneak him
into the king's castle.
But first, he created special weapons.
Ruber poured a magic potion
in a well near the house.
His soldiers and Juliana's farm animals
were thrown into the well,
along with their weapons.
Each man and animal became
a weapon called a "Minion."
One Minion, created from a rooster,
had an ax for a beak.
He was called Bladebeak.

While Ruber made his Minions,
Kayley saw her chance to escape.
She hid behind a rock,
just as Ruber's Griffin swooped down.

"You lost Excalibur?!" cried Ruber.

"I was attacked by a falcon,"
said the Griffin. "The sword fell into
the Forbidden Forest."
The Forbidden Forest. . . , thought Kayley.
*I must find Excalibur and return it
to King Arthur.*

Kayley raced toward the road.
"After her!" shouted Ruber to two
of his Minions.
One Minion stayed behind to guard
Juliana.
"And you," Ruber said to the Griffin,
"lead me to Excalibur."

CHAPTER TWO
The Forbidden Forest

A frightened Kayley made her way
through the Forbidden Forest.
Plants and trees moved like snakes.
Even the mud seemed to be alive.
Then, without warning, Kayley became
trapped in a net.
The Minions surrounded her.
"Hey!" said a voice. "That's my net."
Kayley watched as a young man
stepped forward.
The Minions attacked, but the stranger
knew the ways of the forest.
He used the plants and mud to trap
the Minions.

"Thank you. You saved my life," Kayley said to the stranger. "What's your name?"

"It's Garrett," answered the man.

Kayley looked into Garrett's eyes.

He did not look directly at her.
Slowly, she realized he was blind.
As Garrett turned away, a falcon
landed on his shoulder.

"Excalibur is here?" Garrett asked the large bird.

The falcon flapped its wings in answer.

"We're going after it," said Garrett.

"Great!" answered Kayley.

"Not you," said Garrett. "Me and my falcon, Ayden. We work alone."

As Kayley began to argue, Ayden flew to her shoulder.

"Ayden!" scolded Garrett.

But Garrett knew he couldn't win.

The three set out together, in search of Excalibur.

Garrett and Ayden helped Kayley through the many traps of the Forbidden Forest.

Then, they reached an even more
dangerous area — dragon country.
"Do you think we'll see any dragons?"
Kayley asked nervously.
As if to answer her question, a shadow
of a large dragon passed over them.
The three jumped into a nest of
hatched dragon's eggs.

They waited until they thought
it was safe.

Then Kayley saw two shadows.

"Dragons!" she cried.

"Where?" said one of the shadows.

"I don't see any dragons."

Kayley saw a two-headed dragon
hiding in fear.

"But *you're* dragons," she said to
the frightened creatures.

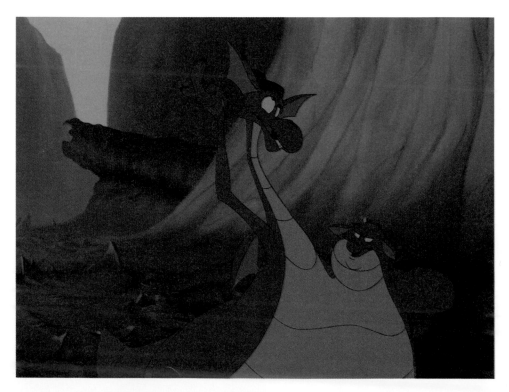

"Please don't hurt us," said one of the heads. "I'm Devon, and this is Cornwall."

"But you can call me Corny for short," said Cornwall.

"Yes," answered Devon. "Short on manners and charm."

Kayley watched as the two dragons began to fight.

Remembering their quest, she and Garrett said good-bye and began to leave.

The dragons begged to join them. They wanted to go to Camelot.

Kayley and Garrett agreed to take them along.

And so, they continued on the journey together.

As the sky grew dark, Garrett gathered the group around him. "Here's where we stop," he said.

"Stop?" cried Kayley. "But we must find Excalibur."

"Sorry," answered Garrett. "No one travels through the forest after dark."

"My father, Sir Lionel, would have," said Kayley.

"Sir Lionel?" asked Garrett. "Kayley, I knew your father."

Kayley listened as Garrett told her about the years he had spent in Camelot.

He had lost his sight as a boy. Though Garrett was blind, Sir Lionel had taught him how to be a knight.

"Any hope I had of becoming a knight died with him," said Garrett sadly.

"He wouldn't want you to give up," said Kayley. "You're as good as any knight in Camelot."

CHAPTER THREE
The Ogre

The next morning Ayden flew to Garrett, screeching loudly.

"Ayden has found Excalibur," Garrett said. "Let's go!"

But when they reached the area, all they found was Excalibur's cloth holder.

It lay in a large footprint — the footprint of an Ogre!

The group followed the Ogre's trail.

The footprints ended at a cave.

"We'll wait for the Ogre to fall asleep," said Garrett. "Then we'll grab the sword."

"Who is 'we'?" asked Devon and Cornwall nervously. "Is we 'us'?"

Quietly, the group went into the cave.

The Ogre finished a large meal and
fell asleep.

Excalibur hung from his mouth like a
tiny toothpick.

Garrett then lowered Kayley from a rock
above the Ogre's head.

"I've got it!" said Kayley, grabbing the sword.

She turned to see Ruber and his followers entering the cave.

Suddenly the Ogre opened his mouth in a great yawn.

The wind from his yawn knocked Ruber and the Griffin down.

Then the sleeping Ogre rolled over and sat on them!

With a stretch of his arm, he pressed the Minions against a wall.

Kayley and Garrett raced out of the cave with the dragons close behind.

Excalibur in hand, they headed toward Camelot.

❧ CHAPTER FOUR ❧
Camelot

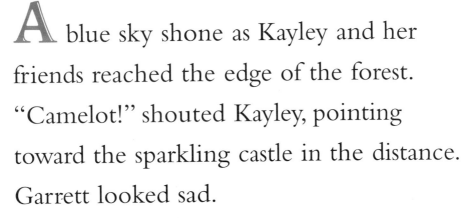

A blue sky shone as Kayley and her friends reached the edge of the forest. "Camelot!" shouted Kayley, pointing toward the sparkling castle in the distance. Garrett looked sad.

"What's wrong?" asked Kayley.

"Take Excalibur to King Arthur," said Garrett. "I don't belong in that world." Kayley watched with tears in her eyes as Garrett turned back toward the forest. Ayden flew after him, squawking angrily at his master.

Kayley longed to follow them, but she knew what she had to do.

She must get to Camelot in time
to save her mother and the king.

The road to the castle was a long one.
The dragons followed far behind Kayley,
arguing as usual.

Just as she neared the gates, a hand
pulled Excalibur from Kayley.
"I'll take that," said Ruber.
Devon and Cornwall arrived in time
to see the Minions drag Kayley away.
The dragons hurried back to the
forest to tell Garrett.

Ruber held Excalibur in his hand. "I've waited ten years to hold this sword," he growled. "Now I'll hold it forever."

Ruber took out the magic potion he had used to make his Minions.

He poured the last drop into his hand.

Smoke swirled as Excalibur actually became a part of Ruber's arm.

"No!" cried Kayley.

A Minion pushed her into a waiting wagon.

"Kayley!" said Juliana from the wagon's floor.

Kayley and her mother hugged.

Ruber ordered Juliana to sit at the front of the wagon.

She was to sneak him into the castle
by asking to see King Arthur.
Guarded by a Minion, Kayley stayed
inside the wagon.
"Don't lose hope," said Juliana.

In the Forbidden Forest, Devon and
Cornwall finally found Garrett.
They told him of Ruber's attack on Kayley.
"Take me to her," said Garrett.
Without a minute to waste, they flew toward
Camelot.

At the castle, Ruber's wagon rolled toward
the gates.
"It's Lady Juliana," said the castle guard. "Let
the wagon in."
The king agreed to meet Juliana at the
Round Table.

Ruber's plan was working perfectly.

But he had not counted on

Kayley's bravery.

Escaping from the wagon, Kayley

jumped to the ground.

"It's a trick!" she shouted.

Instantly, King Arthur's knights

were everywhere.

The Minions rushed toward them.

"Attack!" cried Ruber, running inside

the entrance. "Seal off the castle!"

The Minions obeyed.

Soon, all of the entrances were blocked.

King Arthur was trapped alone

inside the castle.

"I must help the king," said Kayley.

As she ran toward the castle, Ruber

waited for King Arthur in the Round

Table room.

CHAPTER FIVE
The True King

Kayley knew she had no time to lose.
But when she reached the castle, the
Griffin appeared.
Minions surrounded Kayley.
Just when all hope seemed lost,
help arrived.
"Garrett!" cried Kayley, as Devon
and Cornwall lifted her in the air.
They flew to a secret tunnel Garrett
remembered from his years in Camelot.
The tunnel led to the Round Table
room.
Inside the castle, the king walked into
Ruber's trap.

"Juliana. . . ?" said King Arthur, entering the Round Table room.

Then he saw his old enemy.

"Ruber!" cried the king.

"Pleased to see me?" asked Ruber.

King Arthur grabbed for a long spear.

"A spear?" laughed Ruber. "A king would hold a more noble weapon." With that, Ruber raised his arm.

"A king would hold . . . Excalibur," he said, pointing the sword at King Arthur.

Though he was very brave, the king was still weak from his wound.

He was no match for Ruber.

With a mighty crash, Ruber knocked King Arthur to the ground.

"Say hello to your new king!" shouted Ruber.

"I will not serve a false king!" cried Kayley, dashing into the room.

Garrett followed close behind.

Kayley swung across the room on a rope.

She crashed into Ruber and the two
flew through a large window.
They landed on the ground outside.

The stone which had once held
Excalibur lay nearby.
As Ruber got to his feet, Kayley tried
to reach the stone.
Garrett attacked Ruber with his staff.
But Ruber was much stronger.
He threw Garrett toward Kayley, then
raised Excalibur high above their heads.
Ruber brought the sword crashing down.
Kayley and Garrett rolled quickly
out of the way.
Excalibur plunged deep into the stone.
"NO!" shouted Ruber, as the sword
began to glow.
Smoke swirled and a light appeared.
Kayley and Garrett watched as Ruber
disappeared.
The light swept across the courtyard.

As the light touched them, the Minions turned back into humans and animals. Devon and Cornwall magically became two separate dragons.

Shocked, the dragons jumped back together and hugged!

Then everyone watched as King Arthur walked toward Excalibur.

As he had done so many years before, the true king pulled the sword from the stone. Camelot was safe once again.

And what became of our heroes,
Kayley and Garrett?
They were made Knights of the
Round Table, of course.
And everyone lived happily ever after.